Benjamin Dorr

A Memoir of John Fanning Watson

The Annalist of Philadelphia and New York

Benjamin Dorr

A Memoir of John Fanning Watson
The Annalist of Philadelphia and New York

ISBN/EAN: 9783337006273

Printed in Europe, USA, Canada, Australia, Japan

Cover: Foto ©Raphael Reischuk / pixelio.de

More available books at **www.hansebooks.com**

A

MEMOIR

OF

JOHN FANNING WATSON,

THE ANNALIST OF PHILADELPHIA AND NEW YORK.

PREPARED BY REQUEST OF THE HISTORICAL SOCIETY OF PENNSYLVANIA,
AND READ IN THEIR HALL,

Monday Evening, February 11, 1861.

BY

BENJAMIN DORR, D.D.,

RECTOR OF CHRIST CHURCH, PHILADELPHIA.

PHILADELPHIA:
COLLINS, PRINTER, 705 JAYNE STREET.
1861.

REV. AND DEAR SIR:—

At the late Stated Meeting of The Historical Society of Pennsylvania, held at their Hall on the 14th inst., due notice was taken of the decease of our late fellow member, the venerable JOHN F. WATSON, the Annalist of Philadelphia and New York. Appropriate resolutions were adopted, and among these was the following, which I was directed to transmit to you.

Resolved, That as a testimony of our estimation of Mr. Watson, and of his valuable contributions to our history, the Rev. BENJAMIN DORR, D. D., be requested to prepare and read before this Society, a memoir of our late venerable fellow member.

We hope that when ready you will inform the Society, and we shall then arrange an evening when the Memoir can be read at our Hall.

Permit me, also, to add, that I have in my possession some letters of Mr. Watson, addressed to me in 1845, and also in later years. If you wish extracts from them, I will cheerfully make them, as they are of considerable interest.

With high regard,

I am, Dear Sir,

Your obedient servant,

HORATIO GATES JONES,

Cor. Sec. Hist. Soc. of Pa.

To the REV. B. DORR, D. D.

MY DEAR SIR:—

I HAVE been directed to transmit to you the following resolution, adopted by the Historical Society of Pennsylvania on the 11th inst., viz:—

Resolved, That the thanks of this Society be tendered to the Rev. Dr. DORR, for the interesting paper which he has read before us, entitled "Memoir of JOHN FANNING WATSON," and that he be requested to furnish a copy of the same for preservation in our archives.

I have the honor to be,

Your obedient servant,

HORATIO G. JONES,

Corresponding Secretary.

To the REV. B. DORR, D. D.

TO

THE CITIZENS OF PHILADELPHIA,

FOR WHOSE PLEASURE AND INSTRUCTION

THE SUBJECT OF THIS MEMOIR

LABORED EARNESTLY AND SUCCESSFULLY MANY YEARS,

AND WHOSE BOOK OF ANNALS

IS AN ENDURING MONUMENT

OF HIS UNTIRING INDUSTRY IN THEIR BEHALF,

This Volume

IS AFFECTIONATELY DEDICATED

BY HIS FAMILY.

MEMOIR.

MEMOIR

LADIES AND GENTLEMEN:—

One year ago to-night, the second Monday in February, 1860, the Historical Society of Pennsylvania met in this place, to pay a just tribute of respect to one of their number, then recently deceased, the Hon. Henry D. Gilpin. A year has passed, and they come together again, to perform a like mournful duty towards another highly respected member, JOHN FANNING WATSON, ESQ.

I esteem it a great privilege to have known both these gentlemen, for several years, and to be able to number them among my friends. And I should do injustice to my feelings, did I let this favorable occasion pass, without saying a few words respecting the opportunities which I had of knowing the first named intimately, and of appreciating his many and great excellences.

Mr. Gilpin and his accomplished lady were the

2

companions of myself and son, in our travels over much of the classic soil of Italy, and among the stupendous ruins of ancient Egypt. It was no light honor to have the companionship of a man of so refined a taste, and such scholarly attainments, in our visits at Rome and Naples, and the places around them, where every foot-step was on classic ground.

On my asking him one day, how he, who had been so much engaged in a laborious profession, and so much in public life (he was at one time Attorney-General of the United States), had acquired so thorough and accurate knowledge of the old Greek and Roman authors. He replied, that he read some one of them daily; and that he had done so for more than thirty years.

We took passage together in a French steamer at Naples for Alexandria, stopping twelve days at Malta, and two weeks at Cairo; visited those wonders of the world, the Pyramids and the Sphinx; climbed the great Pyramid of Cheops, and unfurled our American flag, with its full complement of stars and stripes, on the summit of the largest and oldest structure in the world.

At Cairo we procured a boat, with a crew of twenty Arabs, to take us four (Mr. and Mrs. Gilpin, my son and myself) to upper Egypt and back. A Nile boat, where there are none to talk with but your own little party, and where you may not, for weeks, see another human being who can speak a word of your language, except your dragoman, who is both guide and interpreter, is the place of all others for fellow-travellers to acquire a thorough knowledge of each other. We had an abundant supply of books and maps—probably a hundred volumes—through Mr. Gilpin's forethought; but we had not much occasion for these, except for reference.

We took many delightful walks together on the banks of the Nile, while our boat was being slowly towed against the current. We visited the governor of the upper provinces, and some of the sheiks of the towns, with our commendatory letters from Cairo. We explored the tombs of the kings, the palace temples of Dendera, Luxor, and Karnak, and all the other colossal ruins of ancient Thebes. And when the labor of the day was over, and we returned to the boat with our minds filled with the wondrous things that we had seen, what a refreshment was it, to sit with him on the open deck, night after night, as the sun went down beneath a cloudless sky, in that delicious climate, and listen to his conversation, always interesting, always instructive.

I think that voyage on the Nile, of thirty-two days, in our own boat, afforded me a better opportunity of knowing Mr. Gilpin than I could have had by an ordinary intercourse with him in the city for as many years. And I can truly say, that I have never known a more polite gentleman, a more accomplished scholar, a more delightful companion, a more amiable, pure-minded, honorable man than he. His memory will ever be associated with the brightest year of my life, —the year in which I visited Egypt and the Holy Land,—for his companionship contributed to make that year so bright.

I have thought that this humble tribute was due at the present time, to one who will ever be re-membered with gratitude as the BENEFACTOR of the Historical Society of Pennsylvania; one who has bequeathed to it his noble library,—probably the largest and most valuable private collection of books in our country,—and, to this bequest, has added an-other, of nearly one-third of his large estate.

But, what is more to our present purpose, if Mr. Gilpin is remembered as the great BENEFACTOR of the Society, Mr. Watson will be regarded as its chief FOUNDER. To his memoir I now respectfully ask your attention.

JOHN FANNING WATSON, the well-known author of the "Annals of Philadelphia in the Olden Time," and of similar Annals of the City and State of New York, was born June 13, 1779, in Burlington County, New

Jersey. Members of the family had formerly resided in Philadelphia. His father, William Watson, was born in Salem, New Jersey, and married there in December, 1772, to Lucy Fanning, whose family emigrated to New Jersey from Stonington, Connecticut.

His ancestors, by both the father's and mother's side, were among the earliest settlers in the two States above named.

His paternal ancestor, Thomas Watson, born in Dublin, but of English parentage, came to Salem, New Jersey, in 1667. He was a man of some eminence, and one of the pioneers of the country, as appears from his being one of four witnesses (the other three being Swedes and interpreters) to the original Indian treaty for lands from Salem to Timber Creek, made September 10th, 1677; and still on file in the State records at Trenton. He afterward had, in 1685, a deed of sixteen acres of land as his town lot in Cohansey, to which place he removed.

A maternal ancestor of Mr. Watson, Gilbert Fanning, came to this country from the vicinity of Dublin, in 1641, bringing with him his young bride, known as "the beautiful Kate," a daughter of Hugh O'Connor, Earl of Connaught. He settled in Groton, Connecticut, and purchased there, about the year 1645, a place called Fort Hill, formerly fortified against the Indians, which remained in the family for more than a century.

This Gilbert Fanning left three sons, the eldest of whom, John, was famed in New England history for his bravery in the Indian wars, particularly in the Narraganset fight, in which he had a command. His son, John 2d, married and died early in life, leaving two sons; one of whom, John 3d, married Abigail Miner, whose ancestors settled in Stonington, Connecticut, about 1642, bringing with them "a vellum pedigree, traced back for upwards of three hundred years."*

These last named, John Fanning and Abigail Miner, his wife, were the maternal grand-parents of the subject of this memoir. They had three sons and three daughters. One daughter married Major Ebenezer Adams, of the artillery; the same officer who volunteered, with Major Barton, to go and capture General Prescott, from the midst of his command at Rhode Island; a deed of adventurous and successful daring, which filled the country with their praise. Another daughter of this John Fanning married a Backus, and was the mother of Azel Backus, D. D., first President of Hamilton College, New York.† The third daughter, Lucy, as was before stated, married William

---

* See Note A.   † See Note B.

Watson;—these were the parents of John Fanning Watson. William, the father, is said to have been "a true patriot, of a noble, generous nature, who would sacrifice his own interest for that of his country." And his wife was a lady every way worthy of such a husband.

For both his parents the son ever entertained and expressed the highest esteem, and the fondest affection. Few, indeed, are the sons in our day who so honor their father and mother as Watson, in his youth and old age, honored his. Of his father he has left us this interesting and touching reminiscence:—

"At the beginning of the Revolutionary War, my father, being the owner of several vessels, disposed of his property therein, and putting the proceeds into Continental money, went to sea as a volunteer, in the General Mifflin, private ship of war, with my uncle, Lieut. John Fanning. They were cast away in a snow storm on the Virginia beach, and almost perished with cold; seventeen of the crew having actually so died. Shortly after, he went again to sea in another public vessel, when they captured several prizes. The only prize-money he ever received was laid out in silver spoons, still preserved in my family as heir-looms; so invested at the time for the expressed purpose of defeating the adage that 'prize money could not last.'

"On another occasion, whilst my mother was a young bride, there being a field call, intended to prepare a detachment to assist Pulaski to repel a British invasion, my father was the first to step out as a volunteer. In the short service which ensued, his commanding officer was shot, when he took the command, and brought off the company.

"On the 10th of November, 1781, his house was fired, and he taken prisoner, by the famous refugee, Joe Mulliner (afterwards hung at Burlington), and by him carried to the New York Provost, where, becoming sick, he was removed to the Stromboli Hospital ship, in which he was detained till the 10th of March following. On returning home to my loved mother and myself, an infant, he found all his patriotic Continental money very greatly depreciated, and himself surrounded by adverse circumstances. Finally, whilst in a vessel, on her passage from New Orleans, accompanied by my brother, who was then preparing as a midshipman for our navy, both were lost. Thus ends the melancholy history of my noble father!"

The history of his equally noble mother was not so sad; many bright days of happiness with her devoted son, were reserved for her. She must have been a woman of rare accomplishments, of a highly cultivated mind, and great purity of heart. We have seldom, if ever, seen a more beautiful portraiture than that which is given of her in a manuscript now before us, written by one who knew and loved her well.

"I can never forget," she writes, "with what delight my childish ear listened to her tales of other days; so full of romance and exciting interest. She almost idolized her kindred, and would weep over the story of their trials and early deaths. She was a sweet singer, a skilful instrumental performer, and a composer of several pieces of sacred music. We have many little sketches made by her when quite a child, beautifully executed; one sweet little colored view on Mystic River; another of the old family mansion of the Miners, built in the reign of Charles the Second, where her mother was born; another a small book of well executed animals; many fragments of silk and worsted work, and samplers displaying Bible history.

"She was also a poetess; indeed, her heart was too full of feeling not to be one. When Lafayette, for whom my grandmother had the most profound reverence, visited America, she addressed to him some stanzas, which he afterwards acknowledged in a very complimentary manner. She was then quite an old lady. Some of her early recollections of New England —a picture of primitive New England life—were presented to Daniel Webster, which he acknowledged with gratitude as deeply touching his feelings.

" Besides her literary attainments and cultivated manners, my grandmother was a woman of most exalted piety; 'a Mother in Israel.' And though her beauty and accomplishments caused her society to be much sought after, we nowhere find her unmindful of her religious duties. A humble Christian spirit pervades all her writings, early and late."

The examples and teachings of such parents could not but leave a deep impress upon the mind and heart of their son. After completing the usual course of instruction to qualify him for mercantile pursuits, young Watson was placed in the counting-house of James Vanuxem, an eminent merchant of Philadelphia, where he was accustomed to speak and write French.

He continued in that commercial house until the year 1798, when he became a member of Macpherson's Blues, which, offending the French interests of the firm, caused him to resign his place and withdraw. He was now nineteen years of age. A clerkship in the War Department at Washington was offered him, which he accepted, and occupied satisfactorily till 1804, when he resigned his post, formed a connexion in business with General James O'Hara,* of Pittsburg,

* "Gen. O'Hara had been Quartermaster-General to Gen. Wayne's Indian army. He was the chief founder of Pittsburg, and knew it, when not one house of the present town was built. He was a man of great wealth, enterprise, and foresight; but was considered visionary when he used to say he should 'live to see *ships built there,*' which he did!"—J. F. W.

and went to New Orleans. At this time he was in his twenty-fifth year; active, vigorous, with good business talents, and an irreproachable character; and all was bright before him. He was soon appointed to the responsible office of commissary of provisions for the army, at all the posts in Louisiana. This brought him in contact with many prominent citizens and officers, and their families, and afforded him an opportunity for cultivating the acquaintance of persons of refinement and intelligence.

His journal, kept at this period of his life, and now in possession of his family, is said to be full of interest. His voyage down the Ohio and Mississippi, in a rude boat, drifting slowly along with the current, for the most part through a wilderness,—with its few enjoyments and many hardships,—is described with a cheerful spirit and a graphic pen. Those who now travel swiftly, and at their ease, over those same waters, in splendid steamers, with all the luxuries of a first-class hotel, can hardly imagine that less than sixty years ago the only conveyance from Pittsburg to New Orleans was a clumsy boat, or a rude raft, with its ruder crew.

Mr. Watson's residence in New Orleans was suddenly and painfully terminated in two brief years, by the death of his father and brother, both of whom, as before related, were lost at sea, with the vessel and all on board of her. This great calamity made it necessary for him to return home to his widowed mother, then residing in Philadelphia; and he accordingly took passage from New Orleans to Havana, and thence to Charleston. The event, calamitous as it was, was providentially overruled for good. It enabled him to devote much of his time and energies to those pursuits which were most congenial to his taste, and by which he could most benefit mankind. We, who are here to-night, are reaping the fruits of his literary labors which he could not have produced, had he remained in his pleasant southern home.

Immediately on his return to Philadelphia, he established himself as a bookseller and publisher in Chestnut Street, and continued in that business several years. During this time he was largely interested in the publication and sale of Dr. Adam Clarke's Commentary on the Old and New Testament, which led to an interesting correspondence with the pious and learned author of that elaborate and useful work. He was also publisher of the Select Reviews of Literature.

In the year 1812, Mr. Watson was married to Phebe Barron Crowell, daughter of Thomas Crowell, of Elizabethtown, New Jersey, a lineal descendant of Oliver Cromwell, the Protector. Two brothers of the family came over from England. One of them, the ancestor of Thomas Crowell, settled at Woodbridge, New Jersey, and the other stopped for a time at New London, Connecticut, and afterwards bought all of Barnstable County, Massachusetts, and settled there.

Mr. Watson's union with Miss Crowell was a most happy one. They were blessed with a family of seven children, two of whom died in early life; five are yet living, three daughters and two sons.* The mother was spared to be the light of their home, the meet companion of her affectionate husband, in all his joys and sorrows, for forty-seven years. She died in eighteen hundred and fifty-nine.

Two years after his marriage, 1814, Mr. Watson was elected Cashier of the Bank of Germantown, on its organization, and held the office for more than thirty-three years, devoting himself faithfully to the interests of that institution. He resigned in 1847, when he was chosen Treasurer and Secretary of the Philadelphia, Germantown and Norristown Railroad Company, which position he held till the summer of 1859, and then retired from all active business, "not wishing to occupy any office after his eightieth year."

---

* The eldest daughter, Lavinia Fanning, is the wife of Harrison Whitman, son of Chief Justice Whitman, of Maine. Selena, the second, is the wife of Charles Willing, Esq., of Philadelphia. Myra, the third, is unmarried. The eldest son, Dr. Barron Crowell, resides in Morristown, New Jersey. He married Julia, daughter of Hon. William Willis, of Portland, Maine. The youngest son, John Howell, is unmarried.

Though at that time full fourscore years old, he was healthy and vigorous; and, as he said of himself, felt like "Caleb, as strong to go out and come in, as he was forty years before."

He had managed the affairs of the Railroad Company with all the energy of youth, and, it is believed, to their entire satisfaction.

For the principal materials of this memoir thus far, we take pleasure in acknowledging our indebtedness to Mrs. Lavinia F. Whitman, a daughter of Mr. Watson, who prepared a well-arranged paper for our aid;—and to John S. Littell, Esq., for many years an intimate friend of the deceased, who kindly sent us numerous extracts from a letter which he received from Mr. Watson, dated August, 1859.

We copy now from Mrs. Whitman's communication, some interesting circumstances and events in her honored father's life, which none but a member of his household could know, and none could describe so well as an intelligent, loving daughter.

"It is a remarkable fact that my father, in his long course of official duties, was scarcely ever detained from his office one day by sickness. Not one of his children ever remember to have seen him sick in bed, till within the last two years of his life. His habits were of the Franklin order,—temperate in all things. I have heard my mother say at the time of his writ-

ing the Annals, that she had great fears lest his double
duties would break him down. Early and late, when
out of bank, would he be found in his antiquarian
labors. This was an exception, however, for he was
usually attentive to the rules of health, such as regular habits in eating and drinking, and some daily
amount of exercise. He was very fond of gardening,
and all agricultural pursuits, and employed much of
his time in this way. He had quite a mechanical
turn, and displayed his taste and ingenuity in con-
structing rustic seats, flower-trays, &c.,—understanding the true art of beautifying without much cost.

"My father was also a great walker. Feeling this
deficiency in my mother, who could never bear much
fatigue, he early trained us all to the use of our feet
and limbs. The Wissahiccon was his favorite resort;
here he would engage in sketching and angling; the
latter, however, without much success. In all our
rambles, his mind seemed to be always inquiring,—
never at rest; and I remember now, that I often grew
weary with having this and that spot pointed out, and
its history told; it appeared to me then of so little consequence. He would try to picture to my young mind
the Indians roaming over those same cultivated fields;
—the Indians I always loved to hear about. He
once took me to see a man a hundred and ten years
old,—who was very communicative about the wars,—

and tried to impress me with the thought that I might never again see so old a person;—Look at him! Touch him! Remember him!

"One of my father's greatest enjoyments, was his weekly tea-visits, Saturday, at Stenton. Here he always found a congenial spirit in the person of that most lovely and accomplished woman, Mrs. Deborah Logan,—the 'Female Historian' of Pennsylvania. He had many years of valuable correspondence with her, some of which, I believe, was presented to the Historical Society.

"One secret of my father's long life and uninterrupted health, was his great equanimity of temper, and patient endurance of the ills of life. He passed through many trials, both of a domestic and pecuniary nature, but never allowed himself to despair. Hope, that 'anchor of the soul,' sustained him. He was a firm believer in an unseen hand that shapes our destinies,—and in the revealed truth, that what seems dark and mysterious now, will be clear to us hereafter;—in other words, he had implicit faith and trust in God.

"My father was remarkable for retaining so many of his early attachments, both for persons and places. He had outlived most of the friends of his youth; but to such as were left, within travelling distance, who could not come to him, he paid an annual visit.

Recently, after an absence of fifty years, he visited, in turn, New England, Pittsburg, and Baltimore. As he never travelled 'without his pencil,' we have many most valuable mementos of his journeyings.

" In every relation of life, my father's feelings were fresh and ardent, as in those of youth. A friend,—the son of an early companion,—in writing to him recently, said, 'It is not by years that we should count our life, but by the soul, the feelings;—if they remain warm and tender, as yours are, we are still young. It is only when the heart becomes seared, that life is dull.'

" My father had lost none of his faculties up to the day of his death. His sight was remarkably preserved, so that he read and wrote often without glasses; and his hearing was unimpaired. Of his handwriting, all know how entirely regular, neat, and free from tremulousness it was.

"At the age of seventy, my father went to one of our neighboring mill-dams and skated High Dutch; and only two winters since, wished to make the trial again, but we dissuaded him from it. He had none of the infirmities of age, and therefore could not feel old. He was a man of the most untiring energy and perseverance, and could never be idle. Within the last year of his life, he had commenced the study of German; being a good French and Latin scholar.

3

"We have several volumes in manuscript on theology, this being a subject upon which my father meditated a great deal. His correspondence with Professor Silliman concerning the Deluge is very interesting. We suppose that no other layman in the United States has been so general and thorough in his topics of research into Bible history as he. We feel that we have a most valuable legacy in these papers.

"Another volume of manuscripts is devoted to the vindication of Cromwell. My father took a particular interest in this matter, on account of my mother's descent from the Protector. He has preserved much of the family history, from the time of the two brothers Cromwell arriving here. They left England about the time of the Protectorate; and, 'in crossing the ocean,' were informed by their American captain of the unpopularity of their name with some; they, therefore, resolved to part with the *m*, so as in effect to make a new family name. The act of change was done on board the vessel, with form and solemnity, casting the *m* into the sea.

"An autograph letter of Mr. Watson to Dr. Adam Clarke, on this subject, written in 1821, was recently advertised for sale, in London, for £1 11 6 sterling.*

---

* The advertisement, cut from an English newspaper, was given to Mr. Watson by his venerable friend, John McAllister, Esq.

"A 'vellum of pedigree,' sustaining the foregoing facts, and giving the names of successive descendants, was preserved in the family, from the time of their arrival down to the period of the Revolutionary war, when it was purloined, with a box containing other valuables, from the house of Hon. John Crowell, in Halifax, North Carolina, by a party of Tarleton's horsemen.

"It was never any effort for my father to write; but he had no talent for extempore speaking, and dreaded being called upon, when attending a public dinner, &c. This may have arisen from his aversion to notoriety; for, though he liked to have his labors appreciated, he shunned publicity.

"And, here, I would remark, that my father was not a man generally popular, but most dearly beloved and valued by all those who had the privilege of an intimate intercourse with him. He was a *true* friend, and his heart full of tenderness and sensibility, was one upon which you could repose with confidence and love. It was sound to its core. His noble feelings were above the little 'envies and jealousies' which so often destroy confidence and affection. Everywhere original, 'he was guileless as a child'— he never professed a friendship which he did not feel, nor sought for public favor.—Had he done so, by being more of a courtier and less honest and sincere,

it would greatly have advanced his pecuniary interests, by procuring him offices of much greater emolu-
ment than those which he held, and which his talents
and original family influence entitled him to. But my
father was not the man to sacrifice personal feeling at
the shrine of mammon.

" I do not believe that, in any act of his life, he
was ever governed by mercenary motives—indeed,
his own interests were too frequently sacrificed for
the benefit of others.

" So pure a mind and unselfish a heart are rarely
met with among men of the present generation.

" It is somewhat remarkable that my father, deeply
as he was interested in antiquarian research, should
not have made it a hobby, to the exclusion of all
other subjects. But he did not—his writings embrace almost every topic of the day. Many of them
are intended only for the eyes of us, his children, and
as such will be held sacred.

" The Annals of Philadelphia, which he began to
prepare as early as 1820, and published in 1830, have
passed through two editions, and are now in the third.
The Annals of New York, it is believed, have also
passed to a second edition. ' The former work,' he tells
us, ' was in effect the origin of the Historical Society
of Pennsylvania; it being founded on a solicited
pledge, that if the manuscript materials of the An-

nals should be contributed to such Society, then it should be based thereon. And so it was done.'*

"The more I see of my father's writings, the more I feel how deeply rooted was his interest in the preservation of the early history of our country. I have before me a copy of his letter to the Hon. Edward Everett, in 1825, urging him to preserve some such history of Boston, as he himself was then preparing of Philadelphia. 'My aim,' he says, 'has been to gather data, which might serve for future exercise in poetry, painting, and works of the imagination. Two years since I endeavored to prompt the New York Historical Society to institute some such researches for their city. Dr. Hosack was commissioned to inform me that it was received with great cordiality, and that my principles of inquiry would be adopted for New York.

"'First aim to give an intellectual picture of Boston and its inhabitants, customs, &c., as it stood at its settlement, and then at successive stages of thirty to fifty years. My scheme enables you to detail much of that which would not suit the gravity and dignity of common history; indeed, I rather aim to notice just such incidents as that omits. I could aid you from a manuscript book of large size, never pub-

---

* Mr. Watson's Letter to J. S. Littell, Esq.

lished, and written in Boston in 1740. I have also some notices from the journal of a British sailor, who visited you almost a century since. You will perceive that the mind, which shall be qualified for such a pleasing task, must possess such taste, enthusiasm, and energy to execute his will, and express his feelings, as must prompt a poet to lay everything under contribution to his art. He must seek out old people, of all descriptions; he must not scruple to act without formal introduction; he must labor to bring back to the imagination things which none can any longer see; he must generate the ideal presence, and learn to commune with men and manners of other times. To prepare a suitable mind for effecting my object, he should seek out, and carefully run over, the oldest gazettes, magazines, &c.; their local news will furnish many facts and valuable hints. Another source of local information will be found in consulting the earliest court records, &c.; but more particularly in the presentments of the grand juries of each court, you will get at the earliest condition of the place and people. I have had some curious experience myself;—and to see your Blue Laws exemplified, in some such cases, might afford considerable amusement to the present generation.'

"In another letter before me, to William Rawle, Esq., President of the Historical Society of Pennsyl-

vania, written in the same year, he urges the Society,
'by its members in every county, to collect from the
old soldiers of the Revolution, all the remarkable incidents, coming to their knowledge, of the war. This
would collect many proofs of individual valor, and
many moving anecdotes. Get also from those pioneers, who were the first settlers in the interior, the
many strange things they first saw, in its savage state,
and the contrast now. Urge the Society to recom-
mend similar inquiries in all the Historical Societies
in the Union.'

"I have made these extracts for the purpose of
showing with what a spirit of love my father labored;
what an earnest desire he had to promote a knowledge of our early history.

"In connection with his writings, he had preserved many valuable relics of the past. His collection is not so large as it was formerly, having recently
parted with many interesting relics and autographs.
He had, at one time, a very great number of the
latter. I presume, however, there are embraced in
the present collection many articles of which no other
person has a duplicate.

"My father's chamber, when near the close of life,
was painfully suggestive of his recent comfortable
moments of health, as he lay surrounded by many
objects so interesting to him. Near by his bedside

stood his old secretary, at which he wrote, containing
his most valuable papers and writings, and by it, that
venerable chair of PENN, made more remarkable by
having seated Prince William and Lafayette.* In
the corner was an old clock-case, belonging to the
same family, with a tray holding seven canes of relic
wood;—the walls were hung round with pictures of
ancient houses, scenes, &c., all framed from some
portion of the woods represented; and from two of
the windows were suspended cannon balls,—placed
there but a few days previously;—one was from the
battle of Germantown, presented by Benjamin Chew,
Sen., Esq. The other reads,—'This Ball is a curiosity.—It is older than Philadelphia;—was found
imbedded in the root of a large tree-stump, in a house
of Budd's long row. J. F. Watson, 1836.'

"One of the greatest pleasures of my father's life,
was to see the deeds of the good rewarded; and,
when they had passed from life, to have their graves
honored. With such feelings he collected the remains of Godfrey, the inventor of the Quadrant, from
a neglected spot on the old farm, and had them conveyed to Laurel Hill, where a neat and appropriate
monument was erected over them, by subscription.

"I think my father's memory was remarkably re-
tentive of all the minutiæ of his early days. He was

---

* See Note C.

then the *observing child.* He says, 'In reflecting upon
the marked characteristic of my mother, in so well
remembering names, persons, and places, which she
had heard or seen in early life, I am led to the
thought, of how much she was like 'the Annalist'
himself. It seems to be a kind of family faculty;—
will any of our children possess it?'

"My father was no great politician; he was born
and died a Whig in principle, though the name seems
to be almost obsolete. He was, perhaps, in the last
few months of his life, the most seemingly interested
in politics, owing to the state of our country. When
sick and fevered, his dreams would be of wars and
bloodshed, and I remember his awaking from a dream
of such a scene as an attack upon the forts at Charleston, and with tears in his eyes telling me,—'I do not
wish *to live* to see our Union dissolved.' Alas, dear
parent, your prayer was granted!

" I have said nothing of my father in his married
relations; but I might say, that Heaven never per-
mitted a union where there was greater congeniality,
or more just appreciation of each other. The greatest
sorrow my father ever knew,—and he had many,—
was when the hand of sickness pressed so heavily
upon her, who had been his loved companion, and
the sun-beam of our home. But I am withdrawing
the curtain from scenes which are sacred!

"Life with our honored father is now closed. We can never cease to mourn the loss of one so good and so beloved; a most devoted parent, self-sacrificing and toiling for us. He is gone; but not without leaving with us, his children, the most perfect assurance of a blessed immortality. He passed away with but one struggle; and then it seemed as if instantly, upon his brow, was written by an angel's hand, *all now is peace!*"

Mr. Watson died Sunday, December 23, 1860, in the eighty-second year of his age.

Here we might appropriately close the memoir of our departed friend, with the silent, salutary lesson of this hallowed death-bed scene impressed upon our hearts. And such would be our wish; but justice to him, to his family, to this Society, and to all who honor his memory, requires that, on an occasion like this, we notice more fully some events and actions of his life which have here been only incidentally mentioned.

From his early youth Mr. Watson appears to have had a great regard for religion. His mother, he tells us, "was a very pious woman of the earliest Methodists in Philadelphia; and her books and her example led him to join her persuasion." In a manuscript before me, he gives an account of his agency in introducing the first Protestant religious services in New

Orleans; by which it appears that he, though educated
a Methodist, but at that time not united in com-
munion with them, or any other denomination, was
the founder of the Protestant Episcopal Church in that
city. His manuscript is entitled " Recollections of
New Orleans," written in 1805–6.

"I was the first and sole person who, at New Orleans, in 1804–5, suggested and eventually realized
the establishment there of the Protestant Episcopal
Church. I first began by writing sundry articles,
under different signatures, for Mr. Maury's paper,
then published there. I was not then a religious
man; but felt a certain 'leanness in the soul,' from
not being able to hear preaching of any kind, in any
church. I had, with sundry others of my contem-
poraries, a peculiar longing for some of the Songs of
Zion, and their attendant worship, such as I had
before witnessed at home. To have no worship was
felt as a bereavement. I was then acting as a merchant, and specially as purveyor for the army supply
of provisions, in all lower Louisiana; and, therefore,
had many agents acting for me at the various military
posts, even as far off as Natchitoches, Ouachita, Walnut Hills, &c. On one occasion myself, with the
officers in garrison at New Orleans, procured the
services of an Irish priest, who preached for us in
English. It was so, that a Scotch gentleman, who

owned the house where Maury printed, asked his
permission to obtain my name, and he thereupon
called upon me, and with tears in his eyes told me
how very much his heart was engaged in the success
of my views; and offering, at the same time, to con-
tribute one thousand dollars towards the settlement
of some clergyman, who should preach in English.
When I found the matter sufficiently ripe for discus-
sion and adoption, in some form, I procured the publication of a town call of English residents to consider
the subject. The meeting was well attended; and
we there found persons of various denominational
bias;—some were of Episcopal training,—some were
of Methodist and Baptist families,—a few were Qua-
kers,—but the most of them were Presbyterians.
Almost all of us were young men, and men of the
world. The first meeting was adjourned for further
consideration; and, in the meantime, I wrote an ar-
ticle favoring a preference for the Episcopal Church,
because it had a liturgical service, and was, therefore,
more adapted to suit the bias and ingathering of the
numerous Romanist families. When we again met,
those views decidedly prevailed; and upon Mr. Edward Livingston's commendation of the talents and
piety of the Rev. Mr. Chase, then of New York, and
afterwards Bishop,—first of Ohio, and next of Illi-
nois,—it was resolved, that Mr. Livingston be desig-

nated to correspond with, and invite that gentleman
to come out and take the charge of establishing such
a church. He did so; and the result was that Mr.
Chase was so engaged. I soon after left that country
and went back to Philadelphia. Since then, I have
myself become an Episcopalian, in Germantown. I
never made these facts known, beyond the bounds of
my own family; and I now write them down at their
request. I was indeed an unworthy instrument for
a lasting good; and now only wonder at the employ-
ment of such an agent!"

For more than thirty years, and up to the time of
his decease, Mr. Watson was a constant and exem-
plary communicant in St. Luke's Church, Germantown, of which the Rev. John Rodney is, and has
been for five and thirty years, the esteemed and beloved Rector. He was a sincere Christian, a devout
man, and liberal in his feelings towards Christians of
every name. He once said, in a letter to a friend,
"a name in heaven is *the* thing after all." And, as
that friend justly remarks—"It does not always, or
frequently happen, that men of his determined independence and self-reliance, in investigation, arrive at
this only safe and most happy conclusion. It would
be better for poor human nature, if there were many
more among men, equally honest, honorable, and con-
scientious!"

A bright and beautiful trait in Mr. Watson's character, as we have seen, was his affection and respect for the memory of all good men who had been useful in their generation. His care for the remains of Godfrey and his parents has been already noticed. They were taken to Laurel Hill, and over them was placed a new marble tomb-stone, with this inscription:—

Here repose the remains
of
THOMAS GODFREY, the inventor of the Quadrant,
Born 1704, died 1749.
Also
The remains of his father and mother,
Joseph Godfrey and Wife.
They were removed from the old homestead,
by Townsend's first Mill, October 6, 1838,
By John F. Watson.
*Vitam navitæ complanavit.**

The same kind care was shown for the remains of a number of officers and soldiers of the Revolution, who fell in the battle of Germantown. Several of the most distinguished of these were natives of North Carolina; and Wheeler, in his history of that State, after recording the names of these men, says,—"The thanks of the State, and the gratitude of every individual of North Carolina, are due to Mr. Watson, for his generous and patriotic liberality to the heroic dead."

---

* See Watson's Annals, vol. i. p. 528.

The same historian, Hon. John H. Wheeler, in a letter to a friend in North Carolina, dated Philadelphia, September 25, 1851,—published in the Raleigh (North Carolina) Standard, and republished in the North American and United States Gazette of October 17, 1851, says:—

" I was invited a few days since, by John Fanning Watson, author of Annals of Philadelphia, and many other works, to visit with him the battle ground of Germantown, which, on the 4th of October, 1777, was literally watered with the best blood of North Carolina. General Francis Nash, of Orange, Colonel Henry Irwin, of Edgecombe, Captain Jacob Turner, of Bertie, and others, fell there nobly fighting in the cause of liberty. Mr. Watson has, with pious patriotism, gathered the remains of General Nash, and erected over them a beautiful monument.

" I saw the grave of Colonel Irwin and Captain Turner. It bears this inscription—

" In honor of the brave.
Hic jacent in pace,
Col. HENRY IRWIN, of N. Carolina,
Capt. TURNER, Adjt. LUCAS, and six SOLDIERS,
killed in the Battle of Germantown.
One cause, one grave."*

* "Their bodies were recognized by an aged gentleman, Mr. Keyser, who saw them interred in 1777; and on their disinterment for sepulture in 1836, by Mr. Watson, the manly form of the brave Turner was still

"I cannot close this letter," says Mr. Wheeler, "without again expressing my admiration of the conduct of Mr. Watson, a stranger to our State and our people, gathering, with patriotic reverence, the bones of her gallant sons, and marking the hallowed spot that holds their mutilated remains."

Mr. Custis, in his Recollections of Washington (p. 203), speaking of the death and burial of General Nash, says: "He lingered in extreme torture between two and three days, and died, admired by his enemies—admired and lamented by his companions in arms. On Thursday, the ninth of October, the whole American army was paraded by order of the Commander-in-chief, to perform the funeral obsequies of General Nash, and never did the warrior's last tribute peal the requiem of a braver soldier or nobler patriot than that of the illustrious son of North Carolina." Mr. Lossing, the Editor of Custis's Recollections, in a note at this place, says (p. 204): "The ball that wounded Nash, at Germantown, killed his aid, Major Witherspoon, son of Dr. Witherspoon, President of Princeton College. Nash's remains were conveyed to Kulpsville, and buried in the Mennonist

known amid the decaying relics of humanity. A piece of the cloth, from the breast of his coat, with the buttons, was still undestroyed. This he presented to me, and I shall deposit the sacred memento with one of the Societies of our University."—J. F. W.

burying-ground there, about twenty-six miles from Philadelphia. On receiving intelligence of his death, the Congress resolved to request Governor Caswell, of North Carolina, 'to erect a monument, of the value of five hundred dollars, at the expense of the United States,' in honor of his memory.

"That proposed monument has not been erected. Private patriotism has been more faithful. Through the efforts of John F. Watson, Esq.—the Annalist of Philadelphia and New York,—the citizens of Germantown and Norristown have erected a neat marble monument to the memory of the gallant Nash, upon which is the following inscription:—

VOTA VIA MEA JUS PATRIÆ.

In memory
of
GENERAL NASH, of North Carolina,
mortally wounded
at the battle of Germantown;
here interred,
October 17th, 1777,
in the presence of the army here encamped.

J. F. W.

"Among the British officers killed on that occasion," Mr. Lossing adds, "were Brigadier-General James Agnew, and Lieutenant Bird. These were inhumed in the South burying-ground at German-

4

town, and over their graves also Mr. Watson has erected a neat marble slab."

"In the North burying-ground, the same patriotic gentleman has set up commemorative slabs at the head of the graves of Captain Turner, of North Carolina, Colonel Irwin, and six private soldiers of the American army, who were killed in the battle, and there buried together."

Having quoted from the "Recollections and Private Memoirs of Washington, by his adopted son, George Washington Parke Custis," edited with notes by Benson J. Lossing, it is proper here to mention that, for these valuable reminiscences, we are probably indebted, indirectly, to Mr. Watson. Mr. Lossing tells us that, as early as September, 1825, Mr. Watson wrote to Mr. Custis, "urging him to answer publicly a series of questions, which he (Mr. Watson) proposed to write; and which," he said, if fully answered, "would go more to develop, as by moral painting, the individual character of General and Mrs. Washington, as they appeared in domestic and every day life, than all that had ever been published."

Mr. Custis promptly answered this letter, assuring Mr. Watson that as soon as he had completed his "Conversations with Lafayette," of which the thirteenth number was just then finished, he should commence the publication of the "Recollections of Washington."*

"Such, in brief," says Mr. Lossing, "is the history of the origin of these Recollections, as given to the writer by the venerable annalist above mentioned, in May, 1859." (p. 220.)

We make one more extract from Lossing's notes, for the purpose of showing who were the McPherson Blues, mentioned in this memoir, and who of them now survive their companions.

Speaking of the death of Washington, which occurred at Mount Vernon, December 14, 1799, Lossing says: "The Congress, then sitting in Philadelphia, received information of the death of Washington, on the eighteenth," and, among other resolutions, adopted the following: "That there should be a funeral procession from Congress Hall to the German Lutheran Church, in memory of General George Washington, on Thursday, the twenty-sixth instant, and that an oration be prepared at the request of Congress, to be delivered before both houses that day; and that the President of the Senate, and the Speaker of the House of Representatives be desired to request one of the members of Congress to prepare and deliver the same." "Pursuant to this resolution, General Henry

* See Note D.

Lee, then a member of Congress, was invited to pronounce a funeral oration. He consented, and the Lutheran Church above Arch Street, Philadelphia, the largest in the city, was crowded. The McPherson Blues, a corps of three hundred men, composed of the élite of the city, were a guard of honor on that occasion."

"There are now,—July, 1859,—only six survivors of that corps, who were present on the occasion; namely;—Samuel Breck, aged eighty-eight,—S. Palmer, aged seventy-nine,—S. F. Smith, aged seventy-nine,—C. N. Bancker, aged eighty-three,—Quintin Campbell, aged eighty-three,—and John F. Watson, the annalist of Philadelphia and New York, aged eighty. These names were given me by Mr. Breck at a recent interview." (*Ib.* pp. 478-9.)

Mr. Watson was anxious that something should be done to honor the neglected remains of John Fitch, the man who invented and constructed the first steamboat which ran upon the Delaware. For this purpose, he wrote the following characteristic letter to the editors of the Louisville Journal, Kentucky, which was published in that paper at the time:—

"Germantown, Pa., Sept. 13, 1848.

"Gentlemen:—I draw a bow at a venture in addressing this letter to you. I have no personal ac-

quaintance with any gentlemen in your place, and
judge that, from your official position you must have
influence with some one or more of your publishers,
who, with yourselves, may feel a generous regard for
the worthy dead who have been benefactors to our
common country. My object is to have your public
journalists, and, through them, your community, interested in erecting some monument near your place,
to the memory of John Fitch, the inventor, to whom
we are so much indebted for the first impulse to the
use of steam-power in the propulsion of vapor vessels,
now so generally in use throughout the civilized world.

"Some years have now elapsed since I began
to interest myself in the name and fame of 'poor
John Fitch,' as he called himself. Before I sought
out his family remains and connections,—whom I
found chiefly in Ohio, in respectable circumstances,—
the public were wholly uninformed of his where-
abouts. Some one published that he died in Philadelphia of the yellow fever in 1793;—another that he
drowned himself at Pittsburg. The truth is, that he
died at Bardstown in your State, and is there buried;
and I have ascertained where his grave is, wholly un-
distinguished 'by urn or monumental bust.' I had
gone so far, some three years ago, as to have laid my
plans to exhume his remains and bring them here, to
be deposited at Laurel Hill Cemetery, and to have a

monument by subscription for one thousand dollars. But while this project was in process, the Governor of your State interfered so far as to beg to be allowed, for the honor of the State, to have his remains rest with you, and the people or State to have the honor of erecting a suitable monument. To this suggestion, deeming it sincere and fervent, I yielded, and since then have heard no more of the subject. To such neglect I, for one, am not reconciled; and therefore I would again desire to arouse some public sympathy through the newspaper press. I therefore would ask that this letter should be shown to some man of influence, that I may learn, if I can, whether this neglect is to continue.

" I ought now perhaps to say of myself, that I am the person known to the public, favorably, as the annalist of ' Philadelphia and Pennsylvania in the Olden Time;' and that in that work considerable is said of the personal history of John Fitch and his invention, &c. Several pages were bestowed upon the subject, and the work should be consulted, to judge of myself, and what I said of Mr. Fitch. Among other things, there was given the intended inscription for the monument, to be appropriated to tablets on the four sides. It was recommended to be placed on the banks of the Ohio ' below Louisville,' where I desired that his body should rest, ' within the sight and hearing of the passing steamboats.' His own words formed the chief of the tablets; among others was this, that ' *thousands shall hereafter traverse the Atlantic Ocean, and descend the Mississippi and Ohio.*'

" I have, I presume, written enough for a *preliminary.* If sufficiently encouraged, I may hereafter give further and fuller explanations. I may say that the conversation of the Governor was not to myself, personally, but to a Mr. Whittlesey, who visited him in my behalf. I have an office in Philadelphia, and reside in Germantown, and may be written to or spoken with in either place. I do not wish my letter to be published, but that editors should in their own way awaken public attention, if they deem it of sufficient importance to *deserve* their interference. I am in no way related to J. Fitch.

" I am, respectfully,
"JOHN F. WATSON."

Mr. Watson was, as we have seen, a true patriot; his family had done as much, perhaps, as any other, towards achieving the independence of their country, while he was yet an infant; and he had seen it attain a height of prosperity under our noble Constitution, unequalled by any nation on the globe. Its UNION was dearer to him than life. We have heard his affecting exclamation, a short time before his

death,—"I do not wish to live to see our Union dis
solved!" And we can understand how deep, how
real, how intense that feeling must have been, in his
great heart, when we read his own account of the
sacrifices, not of property only, but of life, for our
national independence, in one branch of his family;
and when we read, besides, the touching memorial of
his childhood. "Few persons," he writes, "have
contributed so largely to the sufferings for the Revolutionary War, as that of the Fannings. The father
of my mother, and his three sons, were all officers in
the American navy, and all came to untimely deaths
thereby.

"The father was captured and taken into New
York, and died in the Stromboli Hospital Ship, and
his body was whelmed in the pits of the Wallabout.

"His eldest son John, after whom I was named, was
lieutenant, and twice captured, in the frigates Trumbull and Virginia, and then drowned. The second
son, Joshua, was first lieutenant in the Randolph Frigate, when she blew up in action with the Yarmouth,
sixty-four;* his brother, a lad, was a midshipman at
the same time, in command of her tender.† My own

---

* The facts in his case may be seen in the Congressional Report of
March. 1836. He left a widow, sister of the late Capt. John Reed, of
the Infantry. a brave officer, who was wounded in St. Clair's defeat.
† See Note E.

father, while engaged at Egg Harbor, as public agent
in making salt for army supplies, was captured by one
of his own men, and, in a refugee barge, was taken
prisoner to the New York Provost, to suffer there
three months under Cunningham."

And now for the account of events transpiring in
his childhood's years, which we copy from a manuscript before us, in his own hand, written when eighty
years of age.

"MYSELF OF THE PERIOD OF THE REVOLUTION.

"I was born in the stirring times of the Revolutionary War;—of course I have a right to be num-
bered as among those of that era,—to wit, on the
13th of June, 1779.

"That year of my birth was one in which the com-
batants on both sides were without any great efforts,
which could inspire much of hopes or fears. The
chief effort on the American side was the gallant re-
capture of Stony Point Fortress, by the energetic
General Wayne, on the 16th July, 1779. The British, on their part, seemed only intent on devastation
and revengeful spite. Such was their predatory as-
sault on New Haven, by Gen. Tryon, and his burning
the defenceless towns of East Haven, Fairfield, and
Norwalk, Connecticut. They about the same time

made their destructive captures of Norfolk, Portsmouth, and Hampton, Virginia.

"As some counterbalance to these aggressions on us, there arrived to our intended aid, the French fleet under Count D'Estagne, off Charleston, and presenting to us for a brief season, much of promise to our ears, but sadly breaking it to our hopes. The winter of that same year (79–80), was called the severest ever known in our country;—a time of suffering to many.

"I was therefore cradled in a year of sadness and dismay; and much of gloom and apprehension, must have sadly depressed the spirits of my parents, while looking upon their two children then born to such a state of peril and distress. Alas! beloved and honored parents!

"In the campaign of 1780, began the fierce onset of the British on the Southern States. On the 28th March, 1780, they began the siege of Charleston, and on the 18th April, Cornwallis arrived there with his reinforcement of three thousand men. On the 10th July, 1780, however, as a set-off, there arrived at Newport, Rhode Island, the Count Rochambeau with his army of six thousand men, destined to raise our sinking spirits. In September, our arrant traitor, Arnold, aimed to surrender West Point;—in October, our General Greene took command of our retreating army in the South, and there worked his way favorably, in desperate resistances.

"In the campaign of 1781, the British are generally successful in the South, and are wholly reckless in their destruction and cruelty. In August, my uncle, John Fanning, Lieutenant of the Trumbull Frigate, is captured and taken to New York;—a sadness for our home circle! His brother, Joshua, a Lieutenant of the Randolph Frigate, was before blown up in battle with the Yarmouth, sixty-four. In August, 1781, the French and American armies arrived at Philadelphia on their way to the South; producing a time of cheerful hope to my parents and others. In September they succeed in driving Cornwallis into Yorktown; and on the glorious 19th October, the dread British chieftain was compelled to surrender; and with him fly the hopes of the British conquerors. Then, for the first time, could my dear mother look with joy and hope upon her child of but two years of age. I was, indeed, nursed in a dark and gloomy day! With the close of the year, seemed to end the perils of the Revolution. Laus Deo!

"'Yet two years had to pass before a full confirmation could be had, to finish what had been achieved. It was not till the 30th November, 1782, that the preliminary of peace had been signed at Paris; and

not till the 3d February, 1783, that the ratification
was accomplished. Nor was it until the 19th April,
1783,—the day of the eighth year of the war,—that
the cessation of hostilities was proclaimed to our
army.

"In conclusion, I must add, that my mother, wishing to identify me with the scenes of the Revolution,
when THE FLAG OF PEACE was hoisted to the breeze,
on Market Street Hill, held me up in her arms, and
made me to see and notice THAT FLAG, so that it
should be *told* by me, in after years;—she, at the
same time, shedding many tears of joy at the glad
spectacle. And now, an octogenarian, I feel a melancholy pleasure, in recording this my testimony,
for the consideration of my own posterity!"

And how happily has the veteran of fourscore years
told this tale of his childhood! What a beautiful
and glowing picture,—for poet or painter,—is here
presented to the mind's eye, of maternal love, of devoted patriotism, of filial affection! The patriotic
MOTHER, whose father and three brothers had sacrificed their lives for the cause of liberty, lifting up
her child, not yet four years old, that he might *see
the flag of peace*, waving "O'er the land of the free,
and the home of the brave!" and as tears of joy and
gratitude rolled down her cheeks, charging him to
note that flag,—to bear its memory in his inmost

heart, that he might tell of it to his children, and
they to theirs in after years! It reminds us of the
mothers of Israel, obedient to the divine command,
showing to their children, as the Psalmist expresses
it,—"the honor of the Lord, his mighty and wonderful works that he had done;—That their posterity
might know it, and the children which were yet un-
born;—To the intent that when they came up, they
might show their children the same;—That they
might put their trust in God; and not to forget the
works of God, but to keep his commandments."—
Ps. 78, 4—8.

We will not pause to consider how great must
have been his grief, had he lived to see that flag dis-
honored. But we will hope and pray, that he may,
ere long, look down from his abode of bliss on this
our land, restored to harmony and love,—the Union
preserved;—and that same national flag,—again THE
FLAG OF PEACE, with its glorious constellation of
stars,—one more added, and not one lost,—waving
its ample folds over a happy people, united by indis-
soluble bonds; pious, prosperous, and free.

APPENDIX.

BY ONE OF THE FAMILY.

APPENDIX.

THE foregoing Memoir, written, and read before the Pennsylvania Historical Society by one of my father's most esteemed and learned friends, Rev. Dr. DORR, the author of so many valuable and interesting works, entered as fully into detail as it was thought proper for one evening's reading, and as such might be considered complete ; but, having been urged by members of the Society and others, to have the Memoir published, with some additional notes, genealogy, &c., I decided to present it, in its present form, with a short Appendix, not deeming it proper that my notes should extend beyond the limits of the Memoir itself.

Did space permit, I could make many very interesting extracts from my father's various writings, all of which show deep research and great originality; also from his numerous correspondence—no private individual having probably had a more extensive one— with the great and good men of his day, and upon such an infinite variety of subjects.

He had many years of valuable and intimate correspondence with the family of Gov. Livingston ; Col. Allen McLane, the celebrated partisan officer of Col. Lee's Legion; Com. James Barron, U.S.N.; Oliver Pollock, Esq., a resident merchant at New Orleans, and partner there of Robert Morris ; Dr. Tiddyman of South Carolina; Robert Vaux, John Vaughan, Peter S. Duponceau, Joseph P. Norris, Hon. Samuel Breck, John McAllister, &c. &c. ; all now passed away save the last two highly esteemed gentlemen. May their valuable lives be spared to a late period !

Besides numerous other single letters from distinguished persons, my father had a valuable legacy left him, by his early and greatly esteemed friend, Joseph Delaplaine, Esq., "a gentleman

5

very cordially beloved and very generally known throughout the United States, among the patrons of Belles-Lettres and the Fine Arts." It consists of a volume of letters to Mr. Delaplaine, from many of our former presidents, statesmen, jurists, clergymen, and naval and army officers.

My father's journals of travel, some of which are mentioned in the Memoir as made fifty years since, compare very interestingly with visits to the same places made recently; and, did space allow, I should like to make some extracts from them. He says of them: " I hope such of my family friends as shall come after me, will take care to *preserve* these manuscripts. The more they advance in age, the more curious and interesting they will become to *them*. It would be silly to suppose they could afford any interest to *strangers*, from the careless manner of the composition, but they may show to some of *my* posterity, the features of a mind laudably devoted to inquiry and observation; and if one of them, some fifty years hence, should be passing over the same regions, they may be expected to be peculiarly interesting to such. ' 'Twill soothe to be, where thou hast been.' "

" To note and to observe" was my father's motto, and one of his most striking characteristics. Nothing ever escaped his notice; and it is to such minds that we are indebted for the minutiæ of bygone times. Elkanah Watson, in his " Men and Times of the Revolution," shows much of the same spirit of investigation, which I see his son notices in a recent letter to my father, thus: " I think *you* must be the very *counterpart* to my own father, in your observation of men and things. I had often thought, even before I knew you, by your correspondence, of the striking parallel between you and himself, both in your labors and habits."

Before introducing any further remarks, I desire to express my sincere appreciation of the many beautiful tributes of respect and affection that have been offered to the memory of our departed parent, both by public bodies and private individuals. I feel not the less grateful, because they are well merited. All goes to bear testimony to the worth of what we have lost; though, alas! " the altar upon which they are offered is the monumental marble."

To the Rev. Dr. Dorr I feel much indebted for the affectionate interest evinced towards us, and for the bestowal of so much of his valuable time in the arrangement of the preceding Memoir, he having had to select his material from numerous papers.

To my father's long known and esteemed friend, JOHN S. LITTELL, Esq., I would also offer my thanks for the affectionate and beautiful reference made to him, in some six pages of his "Memoir of Major Wm. Jackson," read before the Pennsylvania Historical Society, on the evening of the 14th of January. It was my intention to make some extracts from these remarks, could it have been done, without destroying the harmony of its connection.

I shall now proceed to give the—

ADDITIONAL GENEALOGY.

To the historian, I know that everything is interesting concerning the ancestry and antecedents of one to whom the public will *ever owe* a debt of gratitude for his invaluable services in rescuing from oblivion so much of bygone days. My father, in speaking of his genealogy, after quoting thus from Boswell, "Family histories, like the *imagines majorum* of the ancients, excite to virtue; it is well to transmit pedigrees to posterity," &c., says: "I trust it is not a weakness to endeavor to look a little into family affinities. Bible example has shown a remarkable regard to the preservation of family classes and tribes. The herald offices in Europe show sufficiently the attachment of enlightened men to these things. Even the Indians, following the dictates of nature, much reverence and esteem the bones and remains of their fathers. The monuments and gravestones, as they exist in all grave-grounds, are so many proofs of an instinctive respect for the fathers and families who have preceded us. To *forget* them, only because they have gone from our presence, is kindred 'to the brutes that perish.'"

The Memoir states, that my father's paternal and maternal ancestors emigrated to this country prior to the landing of Penn upon our shores. We have in possession the original grant of land made to the first Thomas Watson, in 1677; also, a copy of a subscription to the building of the Presbyterian church at Greenwich, in 1735, to which William Watson is one of three subscribers, together with some interesting matter connected with the name of Watson in Europe. Of his ancestry, on the paternal side, my father did not possess a very connected account, after their first settlement here. He seems to have been the only one of this branch of the Watsons to perpetuate his name—my grandfather having been left an orphan at an early age, without any near relative, save an only sister, who died soon after her marriage.

I will now make an extract from my grandmother's journal, regarding her paternal ancestor, Gilbert Fanning, mentioned by Dr. Dorr :—

"This Gilbert Fanning was from the vicinity of Dublin, which city he left in the winter of 1641, in consequence of the famous Irish rebellion and massacre, in which upwards of 100,000 English and Protestants were inhumanly butchered by the Irish papists, under Sir Phelim O'Neale. Dublin alone made its defence, by having timely information of the conspiracy. The Scotch colonies were at first spared by the rebels, because they claimed original descent from that nation, and as Gilbert was of Scotch descent, he obtained refuge in that city; from thence he embarked for Portsmouth, England, and then sailed for America, &c. It is said that the family name originated in Wales, that part emigrated to Scotland, and from thence to Ireland. The name is now numerous about Perth and Dublin.

Sir William Bethune, head of the herald office in Dublin, sends to a daughter of General Fanning in London, written notices of the family, which appear in the ancient records, commencing more than six hundred years since. He adds: "Few families can exhibit such testimony of their antiquity."

Here follows a finely executed drawing by my grandmother of the "Family Arms."

A granddaughter of this Gilbert Fanning, I might perhaps mention, as some New England descendant of the present day may remember to have heard of her, as "Aunt Packer." "She was famous for her pride, accomplishments, and understanding." Her husband was Capt. Packer, a descendant of Col. Packer, of England, who had a troop of horse of his own raising in Cromwell's army in 1658.

Capt. Nathaniel Fanning, who died in 1805, was a cousin of my father's. He had been a midshipman in Paul Jones' celebrated action with the Serapis, and received the written commendation of his commander for his gallantry. He was afterwards commander of various private ships of war out of France, and his memoirs, as published, gives the most stirring and exciting accounts of successful and adventurous daring. He had a brother, also commander of a private vessel of war, wherein he was soon captured and died shortly after. Another brother, Capt. Edmund Fanning, whose successful "Voyages round the World" have been published, had command of a Corvette Letter of Marque in the Pacific, where he discovered four important islands, which he named Washington, Fanning, Briutnels, and Williams. He was also the useful projector of the scheme of the late polar exploration to the South Seas.

Another cousin of my father's was Col. A. C. W. Fanning, of the United States Artillery. He died in 1846. Had attained four brevets, and was a distinguished scholar, as well as soldier. He with Col. Thayer and one other were selected by the United States and sent to France to study military tactics. He had been engaged in the Florida wars, which had much injured his health; was in twenty-six sanguinary battles, had lost one arm (I think), when aid-de-camp to Gen. Pike.

"Blackwood" published a series of extracts from "A Campaign in Texas," describing the terrific struggle in 1835, between Texas and Mexico, and the treacherous massacre at San Jacinto, of Col. Fanning (of Savannah) and his men, by order of Santa Anna.

All of the Fannings hitherto spoken of, here and in the Memoir, were great patriots. There were others who adhered to the cause of the Royalists during the Revolutionary contest. We shall speak of but one other, Major-General Fanning, of the British army—a distinguished officer and greatly beloved by his companions in arms—of whom the "Gentleman's Magazine" for 1818 says, "the world contained no better man;" but we know, however, that he had his enemies on account of his great loyalty.

I will close with an extract from Wheeler, the historian of North Carolina. "Col. Edmund Fanning (afterwards Major-

General) was a native of New York, and a distinguished tory. He was talented and finely educated, having graduated at Yale College in 1757, with distinction, and in after years had the degree of LL. D. conferred upon him by the same. He was member of the Legislature of North Carolina for many years, under the colonial government, and register of the county. In 1782, he was surveyor-general of New York; afterwards removed to Nova Scotia, and was councillor and lieutenant of that province. In 1786, he was appointed governor of Prince Edward's Island, which position he held for nineteen years, and a general in the British army. He died in London, in 1818, leaving one son, Frederic Augustus (Capt. in the army, since dead), and three daughters, two of whom are now living in England, married to gentlemen of rank; one is the wife of Capt. Bentwick Cumberland, nephew of the late Lord Edward Bentwick."

The late Hon. John Wickham, of Richmond, Va., the distinguished orator and lawyer, was a nephew of Major-Gen. Fanning.

Further particulars concerning the Fannings can be learned by reference to "Onderdonk's Revolutionary Incidents on Long Island," "Lossing's Field Book of the Revolution," "Wheeler's History of North Carolina," "Lee's Memoirs," &c.

LETTER FROM THE VENERABLE DR. HOLYOKE.

[I make a copy of this letter, because it was written by Dr. Holyoke himself, on the very day on which he was *one hundred years old*. It is seldom that we have an opportunity of reading the feelings of so aged a person, penned by themselves. It is also interesting as showing one of my father's modes of gleaning information concerning the past.]

SALEM (MASS.), 13th Aug. 1828.

SIR:—

I received your much esteemed favor last September, and wish it was in my power to give you an answer, in any degree adequate to your request, but the circle of my observation has been so limited (for the last 75 years I have but twice been thirty miles from home), and the business of my profession has so engrossed my attention, that much cannot be expected from me.

I was born at Marblehead, three or four miles from Salem,

Aug. 1st, O. S. 1728, and in July, 1732, I well remember the funeral of a lady from the next door—this is the first thing I distinctly remember.

Funerals were in that day extravagantly expensive. Gold rings to each of the bearers, to the physician, the ministers, &c. White stiff-topped gloves in abundance. Wine handed about to the company in tankards; many times when the family could ill-afford it. This extravagance occasioned the enacting sumptuary laws, which, though they checked, did not entirely suppress the evil, till the commencement of the Revolutionary War. Since which time, I think none can complain of extravagance of our funerals.

About the year 1735 square-toed shoes were growing out of fashion—few, or none I believe, except old men, wore such after 1737. Buckles instead of shoe strings were worn by fashionable men as long ago as I can remember, but were not universally adopted in the country towns till 1741 or 42.

In the autumn of 1735 or 6 I, for the first time, saw a northern light, but totally different from the many I have seen since. The whole northeast quarter of the sky was suffused with a deep blood red uniform color, without the least variety, and without any corruscations. Since this, I have seen many appearances of auroras, two of which were remarkable for their beauty and magnificence. The first appeared about the year 1754, the second twenty or thirty years after. The first was the most brilliant; I can give but an indifferent conception of it. Imagine the whole northern region of the heavens covered with a bright, luminous appearance of the prismatic colors, green, yellow, orange, red (but no blue) stripes, shooting from a dark cloud low in the horizon, upwards to the zenith, all in continual motion, corruscating with the rapidity of lightning, and when arrived at the zenith, appeared as if reverberated from above, like flame from the top of an oven, and taking a spiral direction, exhibited a grand and sublime phenomenon. The light it gave was so bright, as to extinguish the light of the moon, then about two hours high, and two days after the full. That aurora could not have been very distant, for the rushing of the columns was very plainly and distinctly heard, as it frequently is, and resembled the rushing of a rocket, though fainter or more distant. The second very nearly resembled this which I have attempted to describe, but differed in exhibiting more red light of a bloody cast, and instead of appearing near the zenith, verged considerably more to the southeast, but the brilliancy and the incessant vibrations, and its tortuous agitations, were much the same.

But, sir, you must excuse me—writing is burdensome, and I have already written more, I am afraid, than you can read.

My health is good, that is, I have a good appetite, and sleep as well as at any period of my life; and, thanks to a kind Providence, suffer but little pain, except now and then pretty severe cramps. My mental faculties are impaired, especially my memory for recent events. But, sir, I am troubling you with circumstances of no importance.

Wishing you health and prosperity, and success in your measures to inform posterity, I do, with much respect, subscribe myself,

Sir, your very humble servant,

E. A. HOLYOKE.

I am this day one hundred years old.

Note.—He died on Wednesday evening, April 1st, 1829.

NOTES.

NOTE A.

This "vellum of pedigree," together with the arms and different bearings created by marriage into other families, is now preserved by the Historical Society of Hartford, Conn., as a rare curiosity. "The family arms is registered at Bath, in Somersett, by Clarenceux the 4th of King James 1st. They were conferred upon Henry Miner, by Edward 3d (beginning of the 14th century), for his loyal services to that monarch when passing through Somersett, to make war against the French."

The Hon. Charles Miner, Vice-President of the Pennsylvania Historical Society, is a lineal descendant of this Henry Miner. In a recent letter, he speaks thus truly of my father: "Your father was a most extraordinary man—his walk in literature peculiar—his researches unique, and of great value, and the results like the Sibyline books, will every day become more and more valuable," &c. &c.

NOTE B.

Rev. Azel Backus, S. T. D., first President of Hamilton College, New York, was a man of such distinguished talents, exalted piety, and conspicuous position, that I deem a more extended notice of him will be acceptable, and not inappropriate, as he was the beloved cousin of my father, and possessed so many of the marked characteristics of the Fanning race. Few men have enjoyed warmer friendships than Dr. Backus. His character was formed on the best model of ingenuous frankness and noble feeling. And the deep and universal grief that was caused by his death, is perhaps the best eulogium that merit could have received, or affection offered. Rev. Dr. Chester, in his Biography of him, one of the most affectionate and beautiful tributes ever offered to the memory of departed worth, says: "The man whom to know was to love—the preacher whom to hear was to admire—the Christian whom to see was to venerate, has gone; and left a blank in the circle in which he moved, that nothing can supply—a star has set, never to rise in the hemisphere which it brightened; and nothing is left but its track of glory, which will fade only in the conflagration of the world."

Dr. Backus was educated at Yale College, and his talents at an early age were of a conspicuous order. Whilst quite a lad, he read the Latin and Greek classics with uncommon accuracy, and great pleasure to himself, and retained in his translations of Homer, Horace, and Virgil, so much of the spirit of these fathers of poetry, that many gentlemen attended the examination of his class, for the pleasure of witnessing his singular attainments.

"He had a genuine taste for Belles-Lettres, and had he pursued the study of them with vigor, would have been one of the most accomplished writers that our country has produced. His imagination was sportive, and uncommonly chaste; producing the sweetest combinations that tenderness ever forms, and exhibiting some of the boldest specimens of intellectual vigor and beauty, that genius ever displays. He stood in the first rank in his class, and received his degree with a reputation seldom attained at his age—those who predicted his future eminence were not disappointed."

It is said that the Rev. Dr. Mason, on his return to New York from New England, was asked what he had seen in his travels; he replied "that he had found one man, Azel Backus, who had a bushel of brains."

His mind sometimes formed the most happy and brilliant associations. Imagery in great variety decorated and illustrated all his thoughts and expressions. His letters to his friends are sparkling with genius and wit, the most tender sensibility and zealous patriotism—"portraits of himself, which none who knew him can fail to recognize." His correspondence with my father forms a large volume, and was prized by him with an almost sacred reverence. From one of these letters, now before me, I will make an extract, on account of its singular beauty and tender regard for the home of his childhood. After speaking of his brother, who "is settled at ——, and I hope will prosper, though a vellum of pedigree will not feed children in New England. Many who have *coats of arms*, through idleness and dissipation have no *arms* to their *coats*"—says: "My mother, I intend to visit soon, and hear the tales of 'other times,' and to call at the house and farm once my father's and mine, but now in other hands, as I exchanged it for an education in Yale College. I will see the hillock that covers the ashes of my father, and experience the pleasures and pains of memory! I have often spent half a day alone, in all the luxury of thought, at this *ci-devant* home in Franklin. Here stood the venerable trees under which I sported; yonder bubbles the spring at which I drank, and there blooms the orchards in which I gambolled in all the glee of childhood. Yonder forest-topped hill is the place where, our negro told me, fairies, witches, and wizards resided. No remnant of the Druids could to me be more venerable. South is the mountain, beyond which my mother told me was the West Indies, whither my father and uncle, John Fanning, had gone. A Musselman goes not with more reverence to Mecca, or a Catholic to Loretto, than I visit Franklin."

There are many characteristic anecdotes of Dr. Backus, which show the peculiarities of his mind, his repartee and wit. Some such were recently published in Harper's Magazine, called, I think, "Recollections of the Sayings and Doings of the Rev. Azel Backus, D. D., by the People of New England."

"If we judge of Dr. Backus," says his biographer, "by the number and respectability of his personal friends, we shall be obliged to draw conclusions highly honorable to him. He never lost a friend; and was in habits of intimacy with the greatest and best men in Connecticut (his native State). The late venerable Governor Wolcott was his early and constant friend. By him he was appointed to preach the Annual Election Sermon in 1798. He was one of the youngest men that ever enjoyed this distinguished honor, and he acquitted himself in a manner that would have done credit to the oldest divine that ever performed that service. The sermon preached on this occasion, in point of ingenuity and ability, ranks with the very best ever published in this country. It is the most finished piece of composition we have ever seen from his pen. It was twice republished in Europe. He also preached and published the funeral sermon of Gov. Wolcott, in 1799, and mingled his tears with those of the whole State, upon the sepulchre of one of its wisest and best magistrates."

"As a *preacher*, Dr. Backus was sound, original, and uncommonly attractive—often his manner was fascinating. He seemed to accomplish every object of eloquence without exercising any rule of the art; and it was as impossible to criticize as to imitate him. His manner was his own, natural and affectionate; his heart flowed from his lips like water." "On one occasion, a time of unusual solemnity, during the session of the General Association in June, 1808, when it was resolved to meet in the church at 6 o'clock in the morning, for the purpose of prayer and praise, the house was thronged, and after singing an animating hymn, Dr. Backus led in prayer. That meeting, or that prayer, no one present will ever forget! The whole scene had taken the deepest hold upon his feelings and roused the whole fervor of his soul. There were many circumstances that united to heighten the interest which he felt. The church was erected on the spot where formerly stood a fort that had been captured by the Indians. Afterwards a church had been built in which Gov. Saltonstall had ministered previous to his election as chief magistrate of the State. That church was afterwards burned, during the Revolutionary War, by Benedict Arnold. The pilgrim sufferers, the fathers of the Church and State, seemed to pass before him, praying, teaching, and bleeding. Here their supplications had ascended; here their tears had flowed; and here their blood had been spilled. Their lives had been sacrificed upon the spot where he stood in peace, and their groans had been heard where now the morning incense was rising. Upon such a mind, bright with intelligence; upon such a heart, melting with tenderness, the facts which the place recalled made impressions of the deepest interest. The contrast of the past with the present had its full effect; he seemed to be inspired. Never was there a finer specimen of the eloquence of feeling and of tears; the whole assembly was moved. It is impossible to convey an adequate idea of the scene; those who were present will confess that the exhibition of his talents and feelings on that occasion was proof of genius and power seldom equalled, and never exceeded."

As we have said so much of the power and effect of the preaching of Dr. B., we cannot refrain from the mention of an event in his early life which had almost decided his divinity studies for a preparation for the army. "After terminating his collegiate course his choice of profession was for the ministry; but he shrunk from it, under a sense of his unworthiness, because he thought that his natural cheerfulness would not yield to the gravity and the discipline which the station required. He knew himself too well to suppose that he could assume manners which his feelings did not dictate; and he was too unpractised and too frank to attempt it. He had no taste for other professions; and while balancing between his fears and his desires—while attempting to discriminate between duty and inclination, his mind became wrought up almost to frenzy, and he suddenly resolved to abandon all literary pursuits and enter the army. While actually preparing to accomplish his purpose, and the very night before he was to sail for a southern fort, his intentions were interrupted by the arrival of his uncle, Dr. Charles Backus, the learned divine, faithful minister, accomplished gentleman, judicious, sincere, and valuable friend, and to his young nephew a guardian angel. More than once he had saved him from what might have been his ruin. The night was spent by the uncle and nephew upon the common, and the result of this providential interview was an entire change of purpose in the latter, and a resolution to commence the study of divinity, and to devote his life to the work of the ministry."

In the midst of his career of honor and usefulness Dr. Backus was summoned to his eternal rest. He died on the 9th December, 1817, in the 53d year of his age, within a few weeks of his two early and loved friends, the venerable Dr. Strong, of Hartford, and the learned and excellent President Dwight, of Yale College. "In the death of such men society suffers; distinguished for learning, patriotism, and piety, science and the commonwealth and religion are bereaved."

The corporation of Hamilton College have erected a monument to his memory, bearing on its two sides a Latin inscription, commemorative of his distinguished talents, piety, and domestic virtues.

Dr. Backus was the father of the late Hon. F. F. Backus, of Rochester, N. Y., and the former Mrs. Gerrit Smith.

I have extended this notice to a much greater length than I had intended, but there is so much about this great and good man like my own father—so much nobleness of heart and corresponding intellectual development, combined with the simplicity of a child— that I must make this my apology, if any is necessary.

NOTE C.

EXTRACT FROM "LAFAYETTE IN AMERICA."

"As we were leaving Germantown, Mr. John F. Watson offered for the acceptance of the General a present of great value, on account of the recollections it awakened. It was a box formed of many pieces of different kinds of wood, the origin and history of which he thus recited:—

"'The body of the box is made of a piece of black walnut, an ancient son of the forest, that once occupied the spot where Philadelphia now stands. Contemporary with the trees which lent their shade to William Penn and his companions, it continued till 1818, spreading its noble branches in view of the Hall in which our Declaration of Independence was ratified.

"'The cover is composed of four different pieces.

"'The first is of a branch of a forest tree, the last surviving of those which were removed in order to dig the first foundations of Philadelphia.

"'The vigor that yet animates the vegetation of this ancient tree is an evidence of the rapid growth of the city, which has risen and become great whilst the tree is still flourishing.

"'The second is a piece of oak, broken off the first bridge, built in 1683, over the little river Canard. This piece was found in 1823, at about six feet below the surface of the earth.

"'The third is a piece of the famous elm, under which Penn's first treaty with Shackamaxum was made. It fell from old age in 1810, but a branch from it is now growing, and in a flourishing state, in the garden of the Hospital, and our fellow-citizens delight to recount the story of its origin whilst protected by its shade.

"'The fourth awakens recollections of yet more olden time. It is a fragment of the first house raised by European hands upon the American shores! It is a piece of mahogany of the habitation constructed and occupied in 1496 by the immortal Columbus. Honor to the Haytien government, which still watches with care for the preservation of this precious monument.

"'I offer you these relics with confidence,' continued Mr. Watson, 'persuaded as I am that it is with interest you receive everything connected with the remembrance of the first movements of a nation that has received so many proofs of your friendship.'"

General Lafayette was indeed highly flattered by Mr. Watson's present. He received it with gratitude, and a pledge that it should find a place amongst the most precious memorials of his tour. To this first present Mr. Watson added also another not less valuable, a piece of the American frigate "Alliance," in which Lafayette had twice crossed the ocean during the Revolutionary War.

NOTE.—It was on the 20th of June, 1825, that Lafayette visited Germantown. After breakfasting with Benjamin Chew, Esq., at his historic mansion, and examining the battle ground, he repaired to the residence of Reuben Haines, Esq., on whose lawn he received the salutations of many of the inhabitants of the town. It was on this occasion that Lafayette occupied the "Penn chair," and received the gifts above referred to.

NOTE D.

ARLINGTON HOUSE, 20th Sept., 1825,
near Alexandria, D. C.

DEAR SIR:

Your favor of the 13th came duly to hand, and for the kind expressions you have been pleased to use towards me I thank you.

So soon as I have completed a little work now publishing in a series of numbers, entitled "Conversations of Lafayette while in the United States in 1824–25," of which the thirteenth number has just appeared, I shall commence the *Recollections of Washington*, an interesting and momentous work to this and after generations. Coming from the *adopted child of Mount Vernon*, it may well be supposed that it will contain matters which could not be generally known, but which will be the more rare and instructive "on that account."

I think of publishing the numbers in the United States Gazette of Philadelphia, not from any partiality to individual publishers, but because that was the paper which, in my juvenile days, I have so often seen the patriarch dry on his knee, which contained his ever memorable communications, his farewell address, and above all, which I believe was first edited by a Revolutionary officer, Fenno, of the artillery. If the editor was not the identical Fenno I have mentioned, he was, I am sure, the relative thereof.

The first number, with the preface, will probably be sent to the Gazette in two or three weeks. It will be headed, "The Mother of Washington," a most remarkable woman, and worthy to be the matron of such a son.

The series will be continued, and embrace all the queries you have been pleased to communicate, with anecdotes and details reaching to the boyhood of the great chief, and ending with his translation to immortality. There will also be published his paternal letters to a most unworthy son, but whose filial veneration makes part, and the better part, of the soul of him who now addresses you this epistle.

The work will be dedicated "to the surviving heroes and patriots of the Revolution."

Accept, sir, an assurance of the respect and esteem of him who has the honor to be

Your ob't serv't,

GEORGE W. P. CUSTIS.

JOHN F. WATSON, Esq.

NOTE F.

Concerning this youth, the youngest brother of my grandmother, she could never speak without evincing the deepest emotion—tears always flowed. He was the idol of their household—a child "of bright and early promise," exquisite in face and person, and of most tender, affectionate heart. As a midshipman in command of the Tender, belonging to the Randolph, under command of Capt. Nicholas Biddle, he saw the fatal action, and brought his vessel safely into Charleston, S. C., received there his own and his brother's prize money for their previous capture of a Jamaica fleet, and was about to return home, when it is supposed he was murdered by one of his men. The money, or murderer, was never discovered.

PROCEEDINGS

OF THE

HISTORICAL SOCIETIES OF PENNSYLVANIA AND NEW YORK.

HISTORICAL SOCIETY OF PENNSYLVANIA.

HALL OF THE HISTORICAL SOCIETY OF PENNSYLVANIA,
PHILADELPHIA, January 16, 1861.

Mr. JOHN H. WATSON,

My Dear Sir: I am directed by The Historical Society of Pennsylvania to communicate to you the following resolutions, which were read and adopted at a meeting of the Society held on the 14th inst.

Resolved, That the members of The Historical Society of Pennsylvania have learned with deep regret of the decease of their late honored associate, Mr. JOHN F. WATSON, the annalist of Philadelphia and New York.

Resolved, That in his death our Society mourns the loss of one of its most distinguished members, the community a useful citizen, and the cause of historic inquiry a devoted student.

Resolved, That his researches as an antiquary, and his labors as a local historian, in departments then wholly unstudied, entitle him to the lasting gratitude of the citizens of Pennsylvania and New York, and that his "Annals" will ever perpetuate his name and memory among those who value the records of the past.

Resolved, That as a testimony of our estimation of Mr. Watson, and of his valuable contributions to our history, the Rev. BENJAMIN DORR, be requested to prepare, and read before this Society, a Memoir of our late venerable fellow member.

Resolved, That a copy of the foregoing resolutions be transmitted to Mr. Watson's family, with an expression of our sympathy in their bereavement.

I scarcely need add anything to the foregoing, as they fully express my own feelings. The loss of such a distinguished member of society, and of one who was peerless in his original investigations, is a calamity that is felt by thousands who only knew him by name, and from his productions.

Be good enough to communicate the proceedings of our Society to all the members of your late father's family. You have, as you well know, my individual condolence and sincere sympathy; for he was not only my friend, but he had been, for many long years, my father's friend.

With much regard,

I am, yours very truly,

HORATIO GATES JONES,

Cor. Sec. Hist. Soc. of Pa.

The preceding resolutions were followed by these remarks, which we copy from the North American and United States Gazette.

" Mr. Jones then spoke as follows:—

" Mr. President: In performing this sad duty, I wish to add my tribute to the memory of one who has been intimately associated, for so long a period, with the history of Philadelphia and New York.

" The year that has just closed has carried with it into the ocean of eternity a long list of distinguished men, eminent in every walk of life, and among them was our late respected associate.

" This is not the proper time to give any extended notice of Mr. Watson, or of his labors as an annalist, for that duty, as one of the resolutions contemplates, will be performed at a future day; but the high regard I entertained for him, and the friendship which existed between us for more than twenty years, call for some expression of my esteem, even on this occasion.

" Long before our Society was organized, Mr. Watson conceived the project of a history of early Philadelphia. He suggested this to a friend who made some preparations for the work, and it finally resulted in the volume by the late Dr. Mease, entitled 'A Picture of Philadelphia.' This, however, did not meet the views of Mr. Watson, for he possessed a mind entirely *sui generis*, and specially qualified for antiquarian research.

"He thereupon prepared on his own plan a few pages of such a history, for his own gratification, and submitted it to some personal friends. Their approving criticisms led him to further research and investigation, and at length his collections assumed the form and name of 'The Annals of Philadelphia and Pennsylvania,' a work replete with the most varied information, minute and curious facts, and interesting details, giving to us, in plain, unvarnished style, a faithful portraiture of our country and its early settlers.

"Mr. Watson was a man of great singleness of purpose and purity of heart. He was the true type of an antiquary, and thought, studied, and wrote as one. He pursued his investigations from pure love for his subject, and not for fame. Yet, when his annals first appeared, he was at once pronounced 'the Homer of his class.' In a letter written as long since as 1845, Mr. Watson said, 'It is something to be an antiquary, if it were only for the love it generates among the brotherhood—all so wholly purged from selfishness, and all so cordial and in unity of object and taste.' This was most beautifully exemplified in the readiness with which he imparted information to others. His collections, so extensive and valuable, were open to all, and his house was the frequent resort of those who were engaged in kindred pursuits.

"'We ne'er shall see his like again,' for there are none among us now who possess the same peculiar train of thought, the same inquiring mind, or equal love for the dusty records of the past. His works, as he himself admitted, have their peculiarities and imperfections, but they were written amid the pressure of daily official duties, and were published without revision. Such as they are, they will ever be regarded as monuments of his wonderful assiduity and laborious research.

"But, sir, I must close, and in doing so, I will merely add that the memory of John F. Watson will long be cherished by the members of this Society, and his name will never be forgotten by the citizens of Philadelphia and New York."

HISTORICAL SOCIETY OF NEW YORK.

From the Historical Magazine.

REMARKS OF MR. LOSSING BEFORE THE NEW YORK HISTORICAL SOCIETY.

" Mr. Lossing then announced the death of Mr. JOHN FANNING WATSON, of Germantown, an honorary member of this Society. 'Mr. Watson,' he said, 'had lived to the age of eighty years, with his mental and bodily powers almost untouched by decay, until within a few weeks of his death, which occurred on the 23d of December last. During a long life, he was temperate in all things; and he consequently enjoyed the exquisite pleasures of a healthy old age.

" 'Mr. Watson was one of those useful men who work lovingly for the good of the world, without coveting, and oftentimes without receiving its thanks or its applause. He was pure in his thoughts, and unselfish in his ways; and he devoted many years of his valuable life to the investigation and illustration of the local history and social life of the two leading cities of the land (out of pure love for the pursuit, and an earnest desire to preserve what, otherwise, might be lost), for the good of his fellow-men.

" 'He was an enthusiastic delver in the mines where antiquarian treasures are to be found, but he never hoarded his earnings with a miser's meanness. Every gem which he gathered from the dark recesses, was laid, in all its attractiveness, upon his open palm, in the bright sunlight, a free gift to the first applicant who would promise to wear it generously, where its beauty might gratify the world. Yet he was not a blind enthusiast, ready to worship a *torso*, because it is a *torso*, but an intelligent co-worker in gathering into permanent receptacles such perfections and fragments of the past as might be valuable in the future. Nor was his life devoted to that pursuit alone. He was always engaged in the practical duties of business, and made his antiquarian labors his recreation.

"'In social life, and in the domestic circle, Mr. Watson was kind, genial, considerate, generous and simple.'"

NEW YORK HISTORICAL SOCIETY.

At a stated meeting of the Society, held at its Hall, on Tuesday evening, February 5, 1861, Mr. Benson J. Lossing, after some remarks, submitted the following resolutions, which were adopted unanimously :—

Resolved, That we, the members of the New York Historical Society, have received with profound regret, intelligence of the death of our esteemed countryman and fellow-member, the venerable John Fanning Watson, of Germantown, Pennsylvania ; and that we offer to his family expressions of our most sincere sympathy in their bereavement.

Resolved, That in the death of Mr. Watson, we recognize a public bereavement of no ordinary kind, for his whole life was an example of manifest usefulness, worthy of general imitation.

Resolved, That we hold in high esteem the labors of our departed friend, in the field of local history ; and that we cherish his memory as one of the intelligent antiquarians of the world whose unselfishness has made them benefactors, and whose careful savings of "unconsidered trifles" have added largely to the treasury of knowledge.

Resolved, That a copy of these resolutions shall be presented to the family of the deceased, in testimony of our sympathy with the living, and our esteem for the dead.

Extract from the minutes.

ANDREW WARNER,
Recording Secretary.

LETTER FROM BENSON J. LOSSING, ESQ.,
THE DISTINGUISHED HISTORIAN AND BIOGRAPHER.

POUGHKEEPSIE, N. Y., Feb. 12, 1861.

MY DEAR MADAM:—

I took great pleasure in offering some resolutions concerning your dear father, to the consideration of the New York Historical Society, on Tuesday of last week. I introduced them with brief remarks; and one of our leading members (Mr. George Folsom) moved that I be requested to furnish a copy of the remarks, to be placed with the resolutions, in the archives of the Society. These, and the resolutions, will be published in the *Historical Magazine* for March.

It would have greatly gratified you, dear Madam, to have heard the expression of friendship and veneration for your dear father, by the leading men of the Society, in conversation after the adjournment.

I announced to the Society the gratifying fact that Dr. Dorr would read a memoir of him before the Pennsylvania Historical Society. I wait with impatience to see it and peruse it. In the next edition of my *"Eminent Americans,"* I shall introduce a brief memoir of him, with a portrait.

I presume your brother has received from Colonel Warner, our Recording Secretary, a copy of the Resolutions which were directed to be sent to your family.

I have lost another dear old friend during the last week, Dr. John W. Francis, who had the greatest respect for your father. I have often heard him speak of the value of his Annals of New York, many facts of which Dr. Francis' own observation confirmed. He was buried in Greenwood Cemetery on Sunday afternoon. * *

Your very sincere friend,

BENSON J. LOSSING.

MRS. LAVINIA F. WHITMAN.

NOTICES OF THE PRESS.

NOTICES OF THE PRESS.*

From the Home Journal, Jan. 12, 1861.

WATSON, THE HISTORIAN.

The death of the venerable and distinguished author, John F. Watson, who died at Germantown, Pennsylvania, on the 23d of December, being eighty-one years of age, is a public loss to the country. He was the pioneer in antiquarian research—the father of local historians—the "Homer of his class," as Washington Irving styled him; indeed, he labored hard to rescue from oblivion the habits, customs, and events of other days, and we regret that his work was not better rewarded in a pecuniary way. As far as honor and compliments went, Mr. Watson was not without his share, and in London, recently, an autograph of his sold for a large price. His "Annals of Philadelphia" possesses a great charm to all who take an interest in the early history of that place, while his "History of New York" is equally appreciated by our citizens. Apart from his published works, Mr. Watson had made many valuable contributions to local history, which, with a number of pictures and relics relating to revolutionary times, have been placed in the Historical Library of Philadelphia. Besides historical works, he left some unpublished manuscript volumes on Theology, which subject he for many years made the study of his serious hours; indeed, a better theologian than was our honored friend cannot, perhaps, be anywhere found. He also devoted pages to

* We have only space for a few notices from the Press; many of the others were much of a repetition of the same.

the vindication of Cromwell, connected with some interesting foreign correspondence. His wife was a lineal descendant of the Lord Protector, which fact will account for the interest evinced by these writings. These manuscripts, with others on various subjects, all marked, however, with great originality and genius, will probably be embodied in a memoir, now preparing by the Rev. Dr. Dorr, of Christ Church, Philadelphia, and which will be delivered before the Historical Society of that city. Mr. Watson was an intimate friend of Benson J. Lossing, who will, no doubt, prepare a suitable and touching memorial to his memory. Mr. Watson possessed a heart full of tenderness and amiability. Life possessed many attractions for him; but when the summons came for his departure, with an entire resignation to God's will, and like the patriarch of old, he was, full of years and honors, prepared and willing to go. We "ne'er shall look upon his like again."

From the United States Journal.

DEATH OF JOHN F. WATSON.

It is with the most painful emotions that we record the death of Mr. John F. Watson, the distinguished annalist, so well and universally known as the accomplished and talented author of "Watson's Annals of Philadelphia and Pennsylvania;" for he was, in the fullest sense of the term, our friend.

Our acquaintance with the gifted and honored deceased commenced as far back as 1828, and during the long period that has intervened from that time down to the present, the most cordial and uninterrupted friendship has existed mutually between us. He was the friend of our youth, in some respects our mentor, and largely contributed with his fluent and powerful pen—over the signatures of "Scrutator," "Bereanus," &c.—papers of surpassing interest and value to the columns of literary, scientific, historical, and ecclesiastical serials, over which we, in our younger years, presided.

The last special token of his friendship and fraternal regards, in a literary point of view, was presented in the gift of a set of his invaluable "Annals," with the following characteristic superscription on a blank leaf of the first volume: "Presented by the author, John F. Watson, to his friend, Z. Fuller, 1856."

> "Remembrance, faithful to her guarded trust,
> Traces upon the heart the faded times of old familiar scenes.
> Instructed in the Antiquary times,
> He tells their tale."

John F. Watson was no common man. He was an ornament to society, a faithful friend, and a pattern of all that is excellent and praiseworthy among men. It may be truly said, a pillar has fallen. In his death the public have lost a most estimable citizen. We deeply sympathize with his bereaved family.

Mr. Watson died at his residence, in Germantown, on Sunday evening, December 23d, after a short illness. He was in the eighty-first year of his age.

The deceased was born at Batsto, Burlington County, New Jersey. Early in life he made his home in the county of Philadelphia. For a few years he was a bookseller and publisher upon Chestnut Street. When the Bank of Germantown went into operation, Mr. Watson was chosen as its Cashier, and he held the position for many years. He subsequently became Treasurer and Secretary of the Philadelphia, Germantown, and Norristown Railroad Company, and he retained those responsible offices until advancing years and failing health induced him to resign them.

Mr. Watson is best known as a local historian. His "Annals of Philadelphia" possess a great charm to all who take an interest in the early history of the city and State. The work has passed through several editions; the latest and most complete and elegant having been published within a short time. He was also the author of a "History of New York City," which was gotten up in a style similar to his "Annals of Philadelphia."

Apart from his published works, Mr. Watson has made some valuable contributions to local history. A number of manuscript works, pictures, and other relics relating to the revolutionary struggle, and to the early history of the city, have been placed in the Philadelphia Library, and Mr. Ferdinand L. Dreer, of this city, has recently purchased from Mr. Watson a large number of manuscripts relating to the same subject.

The deceased was the father of the school of local historians who have done so much within the last half century to rescue from oblivion the early history of Philadelphia. The intelligence of his death will cause a general feeling of regret.

Mr. Watson has left five children to deplore their loss, three daughters and two sons; of the former, Mrs. Harrison Whitman, the accomplished lady to whom was committed the pleasing duty, some years since, of christening the sloop of war Germantown, at her launch, is one.

Honor to his memory. Requiescat en pace.

From the Evening Bulletin.

DEATH OF MR. WATSON, THE ANNALIST.

We regret to announce the death of Mr. John F. Watson, so well known as the author of "Watson's Annals of Philadelphia." Mr. Watson died at his residence, at Germantown, last night, after a short illness. He was in the eighty-first year of his age. The deceased was born at Batsto, Burlington County, New Jersey. Early in life he made his home in the county of Philadelphia. For a few years he was a bookseller upon Chestnut Street. When the Bank of Germantown went into operation Mr. Watson was chosen as its Cashier, and he held the position for many years. He subsequently became Treasurer and Secretary of the Philadelphia, Germantown, and Norristown Railroad Company, and he retained those responsible offices until advancing years and failing health induced him to resign them.

. Mr Watson is best known as a local historian. His "Annals of Philadelphia" possess a great charm to all who take an interest in the early history of the city and State. The work has passed through several editions, the latest and most complete and elegant having been published within a short time. He was also the author of a "History of New York City," which was got up in a style similar to his "Annals of Philadelphia."

Apart from his published works, Mr. Watson has made some valuable contributions to local history. A number of manuscript works, pictures, and other relics relating to the revolutionary struggle, and to the early history of the city, have been placed in the

Philadelphia Library, and Mr. Ferdinand L. Dreer, of this city, has recently purchased from Mr. Watson a large number of manuscripts relating to the same subject.

The deceased was the father of the school of local historians who have done so much within the last half century to rescue from oblivion the early history of Philadelphia. The intelligence of his death will cause a general feeling of regret.

From the Manayunk Star.

DEATH OF JOHN F. WATSON, THE ANNALIST.

We regret to announce the death of John F. Watson, of Germantown. He departed this life on Sunday, the 23d instant, after an illness of about two weeks, in the eighty-first year of his age. His funeral took place on Wednesday, the 26th, at 3 o'clock P. M. His remains were taken to St. Luke's Church, and interred in the burial-ground adjoining. The burial service was read by the Rev. Mr. Rodney, the rector, aided by the Rev. Mr. Morris, his assistant, and the Rev. Dr. Dorr, of Christ Church, Philadelphia.

Mr. Watson had long occupied a prominent position before the public, and as the author of "Watson's Annals of Philadelphia," he enjoyed a popularity both far and near. He was born at Batsto, Burlington County, N. J., and in early life settled in Philadelphia, being engaged at one time in mercantile pursuits. He was also employed under Government as a translator. At an early age he exhibited a fondness for observing and noting "men and things," and this taste was fostered by his forming one of a party that went down the Ohio River from Pittsburg in 1803 or 4. The voyage was made, if we remember correctly, in a sloop, the first that had ever passed down the river. During this trip he kept a journal of what occurred, and ever afterwards, when he visited a new place or made a journey, he kept a diary of passing events.

When the Bank of Germantown was organized in 1814, he was elected its first Cashier, and occupied the same position until 1847, a period of thirty-three years, when he resigned, and was soon afterwards chosen Secretary and Treasurer of the Philadelphia, Germantown, and Norristown Railroad Company. Failing health led him to resign this post in 1859, since which he has resided either at Germantown or in Philadelphia.

It was while he was cashier of the bank that he collected, compiled, and wrote his "Annals of Philadelphia," a work that will long be prized by all who wish to know how our early settlers lived and what progress has been made by their descendants; a work, too, that will hand down to succeeding generations the name of its venerable author. Mr. Watson also wrote "Annals of Olden Time in New York," and was, at the time of his death, about to issue a new edition of the latter work.

As a public officer Mr. Watson ever bore a high reputation for correctness, probity, and assiduity. In his private and social relations he was most highly esteemed by those who knew him well, and he was always happy to impart information from his vast and varied stores of facts to those who sought it. As a husband he was devoted, and as a father he was most tenderly beloved.

He has lived to a good old age, enjoyed the honors of this world for many years, and when on his dying bed, he felt that to him death had no terrors, for in years gone by he had put faith in Jesus Christ. He had been for many years a communicant of the Episcopal Church, but he was no sectarian, and frequently worshipped with other Christians.

The death of such an one causes a feeling of sadness, for there were few like him, and now that he has gone away from us, we feel his loss all the more keenly. But though dead he speaketh, and he will continue to speak to future generations of Pennsylvania, as long as the "Annals" are read.